the notorious mr. darcy
A PRIDE AND PREJUDICE VARIATION

KIERA MONTCLAIRE

Copyright © 2024 by Blue Flowers Press

All rights reserved.

No part of this book may be reproduced in any form or by any electronic or mechanical means, including information storage and retrieval systems, without written permission from the author, except for the use of brief quotations in a book review.

ONE
elizabeth

THE DAY the Meryton militia regiment marched into our humble village was one that promised alteration in many a local heart and hearth. The crisp autumn air buzzed with an energy that seemed to animate even the leaves as they danced along the cobblestones, heralding a season of change. From my vantage point at the parlor window, I witnessed the transformation of our sleepy town into a hive of anticipation, as faces both young and old pressed against the glass of their respective abodes to catch a glimpse of the red-coated soldiers.

"La! What handsome figures they cut!" Lydia exclaimed, her nose practically flattened against the pane in her eagerness.

I could not help but smile at the zealous flutterings of my younger sisters. My own heart, though not immune to the excitement, maintained a more measured beat. "Indeed, they are quite the spectacle," I agreed, turning from the window to face the room, where my mother presided over the scene with a fervor matched only by Lydia's.

"Think of the dances, the balls—the officers must be in want of partners! And what lady here would deny such gallant gentlemen?" Mama said, clasping her hands before her as if in prayer to the patron saint of matrimonial prospects.

"Surely, Mama, you do not suggest we throw ourselves at these men like scones at tea," I chided gently.

"Elizabeth, do not tease your mother so. You know very well the importance of this opportunity," Jane interjected. She cast a placid look towards our mother, who fluttered about the room, already lost in dreams of grand alliances.

"Opportunity it may be," I conceded, "but let us not forget ourselves in the thrill of scarlet uniforms."

"Speak for yourself, Lizzy," Kitty chimed in, now joining Lydia at the window. "I shall dance every dance at the Regimental Welcome Ball, mark my words!"

"Pray, save a few partners for the rest of us," I laughed, yet within me stirred a curiosity for the coming event. The prospect of new company was indeed enticing, and I wondered what characters might emerge from amidst the ranks of redcoats.

"Papa will surely be pleased to see such spirits in his daughters," Jane said, sharing a knowing glance with me. Our father valued the liveliness of mind above all else, and while he may jest at the expense of our mother's match-making schemes, I was not certain that he too enjoyed the vibrancy the militia brought to Meryton.

"Come, girls, we must prepare our finest gowns for the ball. We shall show the officers the very best of Hertfordshire's charms!" With a decisive nod, Mama ushered my sisters upstairs, leaving Jane and me a moment of reprieve.

"Indeed, Jane, it shall be an evening to remember," I mused.

* * *

THE BALLROOM of the Meryton assembly was alight with a myriad of candles, their glow casting a warm radiance over the blushing cheeks and glossy curls of young ladies who fluttered like exotic birds among the officers' scarlet coats. The air was suffused with the sound of laughter mingling with lively music, while the scent of roses and beeswax filled the air.

"Elizabeth, have you seen such a collection of finery?" Jane murmured to me, her eyes wide with the novelty of it all.

"Indeed, every stitch and ribbon on parade," I replied, my gaze sweeping across the room where the local gentry had gathered in hopes of making illustrious acquaintances.

It was then that I noticed an officer whose charm seemed to eclipse even the brilliant shine of his regimentals. His engaging conversation had already drawn a small audience which included my two youngest sisters, and his warm smile suggested a convivial nature as he recounted tales of adventures I could scarcely imagine.

Kitty darted away from the crowd toward me, grabbed hold of my arm and dragged me toward the officers. "Lizzy," she said breathlessly, "you must meet Mr. Wickham—he has only just arrived in Meryton to join the regiment!"

I could not mistake Lydia's scowl as Kitty brought me to the group and introduced me to the gathered gentlemen.

"Dear Mr. Wickham, you must meet my sister, Lizzy," Kitty exclaimed.

"Miss Bennet," he said, turning towards me with a bow that matched the elegance of his words. "Might I persuade you to join our little circle? Your sisters speak most highly of you. And I daresay I did not know that a single family could be so blessed with such engaging and charming daughters."

"Sir, you flatter us," I returned with a lightness in my tone, stepping closer. "I fear your informants have been too generous in their praise."

"Surely not," he countered, his eyes twinkling with mirth.

"For I see before me a young lady whose charms should be the subject of much favorable discourse."

"Then I must beware, for such talk often heralds a disappointment," I quipped, finding myself ensnared by the playful challenge of parrying his compliments.

"Disappointment, Miss Bennet?" Wickham feigned incredulity. "That is a word ill-suited to the present company, unless, of course, you refer to the scarcity of refreshments." He glanced mischievously toward the crowded refreshment table.

"Ah, therein lies the true tragedy of the evening," I agreed, laughing softly. "One can only hope the supper will redeem itself."

"Hope springs eternal," he mused. "But if we are doomed to be disappointed, might we find solace in good conversation?"

"Solace is ever found in good company, Mr. Wickham," I said, meeting his gaze with an earnestness that surprised even myself. "And I am most willing to partake in such a consolation."

We continued thus, exchanging witticisms that danced as nimbly as the couples around us, each phrase a step in a conversational minuet. There was an undeniable spark of intellectual stimulation—a meeting of minds that promised the enchantment of friendship or perhaps something deeper still.

The anticipation of the Regimental Welcome Ball had been palpable throughout the day, but it was the unexpected arrival of Mr. Bingley and Mr. Darcy that sent a hushed wave through the assembly room. I felt Jane's fingers tighten gently around my own as we stood among the clusters of our neighbors, all craning their necks for a better view.

"Look, Lizzy," whispered Jane, her voice barely rising above the soft crescendo of whispers and rustling silks. "Mr. Bingley looks every bit as amiable as mama described."

I followed her gaze as Mr. Bingley entered with a congenial

smile and affable nods to several attendees. Beside him, towering in both stature and presence, was Mr. Darcy. His austere countenance seemed etched from stone, and a ripple of murmurs followed his wake like the faintest of shadows.

"Indeed, Jane," I replied, my eyes lingering on Mr. Darcy. "And his friend... Mr. Darcy, is it not? He has the look of a man who finds little pleasure in such an occasion."

"Perhaps he is simply unaccustomed to country society," Jane suggested, her charitable nature ever inclined to find excuses for others.

"Or perhaps he disdains it altogether," I mused, watching as Mr. Darcy's gaze swept over the gathering with an air of detached appraisal. There was an economy to his movements—a precision that hinted at a nature more deliberate than modest.

"Elizabeth," cautioned Jane, "we ought not judge a gentleman so harshly on first impressions."

"Nor should we be blinded by fine eyes and a handsome face," I retorted, though my heart secretly disagreed. For all that Mr. Darcy's demeanor was cold, there was a gravity to him that intrigued me. His eyes, when they met mine for the briefest of moments, were deep and perceptive.

"See how he observes everything," I whispered to Jane, leaning closer so that my words would not carry. "As if he seeks to unravel each thread of frivolity and find the tapestry's worth."

"Perhaps he does," Jane agreed softly. "And what of Mr. Wickham? Do you not find him agreeable?"

"Agreeable?" I echoed, smiling despite myself. "He is charm personified. Yet one cannot help but wonder about a man who shines so brightly—whether the light is pure or mere reflection."

"Elizabeth, you are too clever by half," Jane teased.

"Only half?" I quipped. "You wound me, dear sister. But

come, let us not dwell on shadow when there is still so much light to bathe in."

"Indeed," Jane said with a gentle laugh, her gaze returning to Mr. Bingley with an openness that spoke volumes of her own interest.

The measure of the dance had drawn to a close, and amidst the throng of flushed faces and laughter, Jane and I found ourselves inadvertently in the path of Sir William Lucas. Behind him stood two gentlemen: Mr. Bingley and Mr. Darcy.

"It seems we shall not avoid meeting your Mr. Bingley this evening," I murmured as Sir William's expression brightened as he spied us.

"Ah! Miss Jane, Miss Elizabeth," Sir William cried. "I shall take great pleasure in introducing you to the newest arrivals in Hertfordshire!"

As Sir William made the introductions, the gentlemen bowed while Jane and I made our own brief curtseys. I noticed how Mr. Bingley's eyes stayed upon Jane and how his smile widened as she met his gaze only briefly before looking back to Sir William.

"You will not find better dancing partners in all of Meryton than you will here, sir," Sir William exclaimed.

"I daresay, I am eager to dance," Mr. Bingley said in a rush. He extended an elbow to Jane. "Miss Bennet, if I may claim the next two dances?"

Jane glanced at me and then looked back to Mr. Bingley and inclined her head. "I would be honored, sir."

"Capital!" Sir William cried as my sister and Mr. Bingley disappeared into the crowd. "Now, if you will excuse me, I must find Lady Lucas–" Sir William's voice trailed off as he searched the room for his wife, and then let out another exclamation and walked quickly in the opposite direction, leaving myself and Mr.

Darcy standing awkwardly together at the edge of the merriment.

"Miss Bennet," he said, inclining his head with a formality that seemed almost archaic amidst the gaiety. "I trust the evening finds you well?"

"Quite well, Mr. Darcy," I replied, my eyes betraying a spark of mirth. "Though I confess, the evening's entertainment provides more than just music and dancing."

"Indeed?" His gaze was steady, probing, and I felt suddenly as if I were a riddle he was intent on solving.

"Observation, Mr. Darcy. It is a pastime of mine." The words slipped out, laced with a challenge. "One can learn a great deal about a person in such settings, do you not agree?"

"Observation can be misleading," he retorted, his voice tinged with an edge. "It often requires a discerning eye to distinguish between appearance and reality."

"Ah, but that is the crux of the matter." I could not help but lean in, drawn by the puzzle he presented. "For a discerning eye might find that the coldest exteriors hide the warmest of hearts."

"Or that the most charming facades conceal deceit." His words were pointed, and for a moment, I wondered at their meaning.

"Perhaps." I allowed a pause, watching as his expression shifted, a flicker of something unguarded before the mask returned. "But one must be willing to look beyond first impressions."

"Perhaps," he said, a hint of ruefulness touching his lips. "But I have rarely been steered wrong by a first impression."

"How unfortunate that your opinion should be so set after only a brief interaction," I said, the corner of my mouth tilting upwards. Before another word could pass between us, he was summoned away, leaving a curious warmth in the wake of our exchange.

The remainder of the evening saw me once again in Mr. Wickham's company, his tales spun with such heartfelt sincerity that I could scarce doubt his conviction. He spoke of injustices, of promises broken by those with power—Mr. Darcy, he claimed—and my heart clenched at the thought of such cruelty.

"Is it possible," I pondered aloud, "for a man to bear such malice?"

"Alas, Miss Bennet," Wickham replied, his eyes shimmering with a melancholy light, "there are men who know only their own desires. Men like Mr. Darcy care not for the harm they inflict upon others."

"Surely there must be some misunderstanding," I voiced, though my thoughts were tumultuous waves crashing against a steadfast cliff. Wickham's narrative painted a stark portrait, yet I could not reconcile it with the man I had just begun to perceive—a man whose reserve may well cloak a depth of feeling.

"Would that it were so," he sighed, and I found my sympathies ensnared by his plight.

As the night drew to a close, and the stars held court in the ink-black sky, I contemplated the enigma of these two gentlemen. My attraction to George Wickham was clear—he appealed to my desire for justice, for kinship. Yet, Mr. Darcy, austere and enigmatic, beckoned my curiosity to unravel the complexities of his character.

Torn between the allure of a charming officer and the intrigue of a proud gentleman, I retired with a mind awash in contradiction, pondering the truth that lay veiled beneath surface and smiles.

TWO
elizabeth

THE REGIMENTAL BALL was aflutter with the kind of excitement that can only be attributed to the presence of officers in their scarlet coats, but it was not the splendor of military regalia that captured my interest so much as the words whispered in darkened corners by Mr. George Wickham. I had found myself ensnared by his congeniality earlier in the evening, and now, as I watched from the periphery, I saw him weave an intricate web of deceit throughout the room.

"Mr. Darcy's character," Wickham confided to a cluster of attentive ladies, "is not so unblemished as his estate might suggest." His voice was laced with a sorrow that seemed too poignant to be feigned, and I could not help but notice how his tale of woe appeared to affect his audience.

"Indeed, Miss Bennet," he turned suddenly towards me, including me in his audience with a meaningful glance, "one would scarcely believe the hardship I have suffered at his hands."

His eyes held mine captive, and I found myself drawn into the gravity of his narrative. There was an undeniable charm about Mr. Wickham, a magnetism that made it quite impossible to look away or question the veracity of his claims. Yet even as I listened, my conscience pricked me; for though Mr. Darcy was a man whose countenance often betrayed little of his thoughts and feelings, I could not reconcile the image of the tyrant that Mr. Wickham painted with the gentleman I had observed from afar.

"Surely," I ventured, compelled by a mix of intrigue and skepticism, "there must be some misunderstanding between you and Mr. Darcy. A man of his consequence would not—"

"Ah, dear Miss Bennet," Mr. Wickham interrupted with a wry smile, "you are as charitable as you are discerning. But alas, I am afraid I have been most grievously wronged, and there is little to misunderstand in matters of lost inheritance and denied promises."

His words struck a chord within the gathering, eliciting murmurs of sympathy and indignation. I watched as faces turned from Mr. Wickham to cast surreptitious glances at Mr. Darcy, who stood aloof on the opposite side of the ballroom, conversing in hushed tones with his friend, Mr. Bingley. A pang of something akin to regret twined its way through my chest, for it pained me to see a man so unjustly maligned without cause or proof.

Yet despite this unease, I could not deny the allure that Mr. Wickham possessed. His tales, elegantly told and rich with emotion, were designed to captivate—and captivate they did. In that moment, I began to wonder if perhaps there was more depth to Mr. Wickham than I had initially perceived.

"Miss Bennet," he said, drawing closer, "I sense in you a kindred spirit—one who values truth and justice. It brings me great comfort to know that someone of your discernment and good taste attends to my account."

Flattery, when artfully executed, is difficult to resist; and resist I did not. For the remainder of the evening, I allowed myself to be charmed by Mr. Wickham's engaging conversation, all the while observing Mr. Darcy from a distance.

As the music faded into the night and the Regimental Ball drew to a close, I found myself ensnared by a peculiar sense of curiosity. The image of Mr. Darcy, so often solitary amidst the throng, remained etched in my mind. Despite Mr. Wickham's earlier narratives depicting him as villainous, there was an enigmatic quality about Mr. Darcy that piqued my interest.

"Is it not peculiar," I mused aloud to Jane as we prepared for our outing to Meryton the following day, "that a man can be both so reserved and yet command such attention?"

"Indeed, Lizzy," she replied with her customary sweetness, "but one's true character is rarely discernible at first glance."

Her words echoed in my thoughts as we ambled through the quaint streets of Meryton. The village was abuzz with activity, and snippets of conversation floated on the breeze. It was not long before my ears caught the familiar name of Mr. Darcy amidst the idle chatter of the townsfolk.

"Mr. Darcy, you say?" quizzed the baker to his customer, his tone laced with disdain. "If he were to darken my doorstep with his presence, I should think twice before serving him!"

"Quite right!" exclaimed the butcher, who was arranging his finest cuts in the window. "A man who deals so ill with his acquaintances is no gentleman, indeed."

The scandal, it seemed, had taken firm root in public opinion, and Mr. Darcy's reputation bore the unfortunate brunt of it. With each passing remark, my curiosity deepened, and I wondered at the disparity between the rumors and the man's own austere demeanor.

"Such talk is most ungenerous without acquaintance," I said to Jane as we continued our stroll. She nodded, though I knew her gentle nature found little comfort in such gossip.

As we returned home, I reflected upon the day's discoveries.

Mr. Darcy, for all his aloofness, had become an enigma that I could not disregard. There was a complexity to him that belied the simplicity of Mr. Wickham's tales, and I resolved to observe him more closely, should the opportunity arise.

For now, the sun dipped low beneath the horizon, and I retired to my chamber for the evening. I could not help but be haunted by the myriad tales and rumors swirling around Mr. Darcy. At one moment, a man of integrity and profound silence; at the next, a figure maligned by gossip and disdain. The contrast was as stark as night from day. My own sentiments, I must confess, were in a state of similar discord.

Mr. Wickham's pleasing manners and agreeable conversation were indeed captivating. I paced before the hearth where a fire crackled soothingly as I tried to collect my tangled thoughts. *Yet it is precisely such a charming veneer that may conceal a duplicitous heart.*

I paused, reflecting on Mr. Darcy's severe countenance and how it might just as easily mask a noble spirit. It occurred to me then that the quietness of his nature, which I had initially taken for arrogance, could instead be a sign of thoughtful reserve—a contemplation that drew an unexpected sigh from my lips.

"Lizzy, what troubles you so?" Jane's gentle voice called me from my reverie as she entered my room, her expression etched with concern.

"Only the perplexing character of two gentlemen," I replied, forcing a lightness into my tone that did not reach my eyes. "One opens his heart with ease, while the other guards it as though it were a treasure chest."

"Perhaps time will reveal the truth of their hearts," Jane soothed, ever the optimist.

"Perhaps," I echoed, yet I remained unconvinced.

* * *

THE FOLLOWING afternoon found us taking tea at Netherfield Park—a respite from the bustling energy of Meryton and the heavy weight of public opinion. As we were ushered into the drawing-room, I observed Mr. Darcy standing by the window, his tall frame relaxed in the flood of sunlight. It was a vision of him I had not expected, and it confounded me further.

"Miss Bennet," he greeted, his voice holding a note of warmth that caused me to startle, "I trust your family is in good health?"

"Indeed, sir. And yours?" I inquired, matching his civility while noting the absence of any coldness in his demeanor.

"Quite well, I thank you," he replied, offering a small smile that seemed to soften the lines of his face.

As we took our tea, the conversation flowed more freely than I would have imagined possible. Mr. Darcy spoke of literature and his sister's progress at the pianoforte with an ease that bordered on affectionate pride. There was an earnestness in his speech that stood in stark opposition to the haughtiness I had been led to expect.

"Miss Elizabeth," he addressed me directly, his gaze intent, "I understand you enjoy walking the countryside. Perhaps you would honor me with your company on a turn about the gardens?"

Surprised by the invitation, I hesitated, but curiosity won over caution. "That would be most agreeable," I consented, setting aside my teacup.

As we strolled through the meticulously kept grounds, the cadence of our conversation was unhurried, and a thought took root in my mind: Could the tales spun by Mr. Wickham be naught but fabrications woven from envy and spite?

"Mr. Darcy," I ventured, a boldness creeping into my voice,

"there are many stories afoot concerning your history with Mr. Wickham. I wonder if such narratives do justice to the truth."

His expression turned grave, and I feared I had breached propriety. "Miss Bennet," he began slowly, "I am ill-equipped to halt the spread of falsehoods, but I can assure you that the truth is oftentimes less simple—and less sensational—than some would make it."

"Indeed," I said softly, my mind racing with new uncertainties. "Truth has a quiet voice, easily drowned out by the clamor of lies."

"Then perhaps it is time I sought to raise my voice above the whispers," Mr. Darcy murmured, more to himself than to me.

"Perhaps," I agreed, feeling the weight of my earlier judgments and wondering if they had been misplaced.

As we returned inside, I thanked him for the pleasant walk, my thoughts clouded with complexity. Jane awaited me with a smile, unaware of the internal tumult the afternoon had stirred.

"Was it not delightful?" she asked, linking her arm through mine.

"Delightful and disconcerting in equal measure," I replied with a rueful smile, knowing that my understanding of both men had become a puzzle I was now determined to solve.

THREE
elizabeth

I HAD SCARCELY TAKEN a dozen steps through the throng of Meryton's bustling market when I found myself face to face with Mr. Wickham, who was in conversation with my sister Kitty. She greeted me with a fluttering wave, her eyes wide with the excitement of such company.

"Ah, Miss Elizabeth," Mr. Wickham said, dipping his head in a courteous bow as I approached. "A pleasure to see you again."

"Mr. Wickham," I replied, returning his greeting with a nod and a smile that belied my sudden curiosity. His presence had lent an unforeseen charge to the air, like the subtle shift in atmosphere before a storm.

Kitty, ever so eager yet easily distracted, soon espied a ribbon vendor's colorful display. "Lizzy, look at those ribbons! I must see them." And with that, she scampered off, leaving Mr. Wickham and me alone amidst the hum of village life.

"Your sister seems quite taken with the array of finery," Mr. Wickham observed, his voice tinged with mirth as we watched her go.

"Indeed, she has always had a particular fondness for

ribbons," I said, turning back to him with a laugh. "So tell me, how do you find Meryton today, sir?"

"Most agreeable, Miss Bennet, especially now," he said, his gaze holding mine with practiced ease.

"Mr. Wickham, I do hope that you will allow me– I have been thinking about our conversation at the ball..."

"Alas," he said with a sigh. "I fear that I have already said too much–"

"Indeed not," I exclaimed. "I would be most grateful to hear your story. If you would tell me– Mr. Darcy has done you a great wrong, has he not?"

"That is true, Miss Bennet," he said after a moment's pause. "He has dealt me a great many wrongs, but none so great as his attempts to deny me my rightful inheritance. An inheritance squandered, no doubt, on his own selfish pursuits," Mr. Wickham confided, his countenance a portrait of wounded nobility.

"Such behavior seems most ungentlemanly," I remarked, feeling the stirrings of indignation on his behalf, despite my natural inclination to skepticism. "And you were left without recourse?"

"None whatsoever. Mr. Darcy's influence is far-reaching, and I was left with no other option but to take up the commission of a humble officer," he said with a rueful smile that spoke of a resignation borne of hardship.

"Thank you, Mr. Wickham," I said, though my mind churned with thoughts of Mr. Darcy's hidden depths and the veracity of the account I had been given. "It is indeed a serious matter if true, and I thank you for entrusting me with your story."

"True it is, and much more besides," he assured me with a solemn nod. "But I would not trouble you further with my grievances."

"There is more? But you must tell me," I beseeched him, my heart alight with the flames of intrigue and compassion. "I have spoken with Mr. Darcy and such behavior seems... quite unlike the character he presented."

"Is it indeed?" Mr. Wickham arched a brow, the corner of his mouth twitching upwards in an expression that could only be interpreted as sardonic amusement. "You must allow me to set the stage for you, Miss Bennet. Picture, if you will, a young lady of tender years and sweeter temperament, her heart full of the purest intentions."

My curiosity piqued, I leaned closer, the better to capture each word that fell from his lips. "And Mr. Darcy sought to take advantage of such innocence?"

"Take advantage? He plotted, Miss Bennet, with all the cunning of a fox," Wickham proclaimed, his voice low and tinged with a gravity that befitted such devious machinations. "An elopement was in the works. It would have been the ruination of the poor creature if not for a fortunate twist of fate."

"Good heavens!" I exclaimed, scarcely able to contain my shock. "And what role did you play in this drama?"

"Ah, but I am getting ahead of myself." He paused, gazing into the distance with a practiced look of noble suffering. "It was by the merest chance that I stumbled upon Mr. Darcy's scheme. My conscience would not allow me to stand idly by while such an injustice was carried out. And so, I intervened."

"Intervened?" I echoed, my mind racing with images conjured by his vivid narration.

"Indeed. I alerted the family, exposed the plot, and the elopement was averted," he said with a flourish, as though recounting a heroic deed from an ancient ballad.

"Mr. Wickham, your bravery is commendable," I said, my sentiments genuine. "I can scarcely imagine Mr. Darcy capable of such dishonorable conduct."

"Alas, Miss Bennet," he sighed, "the man you see before you in society bears little resemblance to the one who operates in shadows. It is a harsh truth to swallow."

"Yet, I cannot reconcile the Mr. Darcy known to me with the villain of your tale," I confessed, my belief in his integrity wavering like a candle in the wind.

"Appearances can deceive, dear lady," Wickham replied, his gaze locking onto mine with piercing intensity. "One must look beyond the veneer of respectability to discern the true nature of a person."

"Indeed, sir, your words hold much wisdom," I conceded, the unsettling notion that I had perhaps misjudged Mr. Darcy gnawing at my conviction.

"Miss Bennet, I trust you will keep this matter close to your heart," he implored, his hand resting briefly upon mine in a gesture of earnest entreaty.

"Your secret is safe with me, Mr. Wickham," I assured him, though the weight of his confidence bore heavily upon my spirit. "I am grateful for your candor and shall reflect upon these revelations with due consideration."

"Thank you, Miss Bennet. Your understanding is a balm to my troubled soul," he said, bowing slightly before excusing himself with a graceful ease that belied the gravity of our discourse.

Left alone with my thoughts, I contemplated the chasm that yawned before me, separating the Mr. Darcy I thought I knew from the one now painted in sinister hues by Mr. Wickham's persuasive tongue. What vexation it was to feel thus torn between judgment and sentiment!

* * *

THE AFTERNOON SUN was drawing low over Longbourn as Kitty and I made our way home, the former's spirits buoyed by her new purchase of ribbons—a rainbow to adorn her bonnet. Yet my own mind was troubled, the echoes of Mr. Wickham's account reverberating within like the tolling of an ominous bell.

I had promised Mr Wickham that I wouldn't tell a soul of our exchange, but I simply could not keep this from my dear sister. I entered the sitting room in a rush, surprising Jane as she sat embroidering.

"Lizzy," she exclaimed, "you look as though you have had a fright–pray, what has happened?"

"Nothing has happened," I said as I sat down beside her, "however, I encountered Mr. Wickham in the village today, and he has imparted a tale most distressing concerning Mr. Darcy."

"Distressing?" Jane's needle paused mid-stitch, her eyes reflecting the sudden gravity that had befallen us. "Pray, tell me what he has said."

I recounted Wickham's narrative with as much composure as I could muster, his allegations painting Mr. Darcy as the villain in a sordid attempt at an elopement. With each word spoken, I felt a chasm widen between the image of the man I had begrudgingly admired and this new, darker portrait sketched by Wickham's skilled hand.

"Can it truly be?" I concluded, the furrow of my brow deepening. "Could Mr. Darcy be capable of such duplicity?"

"Elizabeth, you must take care," Jane replied with characteristic caution, her voice a gentle balm to my agitation. "We know not the full measure of either gentleman's character, and it is unwise to cast judgment without proper evidence."

"Indeed," I conceded, folding my hands in my lap, feeling them tremble slightly. "But Mr. Wickham seemed so genuine in his distress. And yet..."

"And yet?" Jane prompted softly, setting aside her embroidery to give me her undivided attention.

"And yet—how can it be that Mr. Bingley, whose amiable nature we have both esteemed, would choose for his closest companion a man capable of such deceit? It seems incongruous."

"Most incongruous," Jane agreed, her lovely features etched with concern. "Mr. Bingley himself has shown nothing but kindness and good humor. It is difficult to imagine him aligning with someone who harbors dishonorable intentions."

"Exactly so!" My fingers twisted a lock of hair, a nervous habit that betrayed my inner disquiet. "I find myself caught betwixt two narratives, each compelling in its own right. How does one discern the truth when shrouded by such charm and elegance on both sides?"

"Perhaps time will reveal their true characters," Jane suggested, the epitome of patience and wisdom. "We must observe and listen, dear sister, lest we are swayed by mere appearances and eloquence."

"Your counsel is most prudent, Jane." A soft sigh escaped me as I peered out the window, the sweeping lawns of Longbourn offering no answers, only a reflection of my own uncertainty. "Observation and patience, then, shall be my allies in this vexing puzzle."

"Let us trust that the truth will come to light," Jane murmured, resuming her needlework with a steady hand that belied the unease that surely gripped her heart as tightly as it did mine.

"Trust..." I mused aloud, gazing into the horizon where the day's light began to yield to the encroaching dusk. "A commodity now more precious than ever before."

FOUR

darcy

THE EVENING AIR was filled with the kind of gentle warmth that spoke of spring's tender advances upon Hertfordshire. As I entered Lucas Lodge, my eyes swiftly adjusted to the candlelit bathed the room in a warm radiance. The usual hum of genteel society conversation enveloped me, a sound both comforting and disquieting as I pondered the whispers which had begun to circulate about my character.

I stood for a moment in silence, surveying the assembly with an impassive gaze. My hands felt strangely cumbersome at my sides, one thumb absently brushing the signet ring—a family heirloom—that adorned my finger. It was not long before I espied her, Elizabeth Bennet, engaged in what appeared to be a lively discussion with Charlotte Lucas. Her countenance radiated an animation that was at once alluring and intimidating.

With a steadying breath, I resolved to approach them, my boots sinking into the plush carpet with each determined step. The murmurs grew fainter as I neared, and I caught Elizabeth's eye just as I arrived within speaking distance.

"Miss Bennet, Miss Lucas," I began, inclining my head with a courteous nod. "May I beg a moment of your time?"

"Mr. Darcy," Elizabeth replied, her eyes alight with a spark of curiosity. "Of course. We are always at your service."

"Indeed, Mr. Darcy," Charlotte added, offering a warm smile tempered by the formality of our acquaintance. "To what do we owe this unexpected pleasure?"

"Unexpected it may be, but necessity compels me," I admitted, my voice carrying the weight of my unease. "You see, it has come to my attention that certain... unfounded tales concerning my past dealings have been bandied about. Tales most egregiously false and injurious to my reputation."

"Ah," Elizabeth interjected, her brows arching with interest. "You speak of Mr. Wickham's account, I presume?"

"Indeed, I do," I confirmed, firm yet somber. "It pains me to think that such slander might poison the well of society's opinion against me."

"Surely you understand, Mr. Darcy, that people will form their judgments based on the information presented to them," Elizabeth said, her tone tinged with a hint of challenge. "Mr. Wickham's story is compelling, to say the least."

"Compelling it may be, but truth holds a higher value than mere theatricality," I countered. "Mr. Wickham's version is a carefully crafted performance designed to elicit sympathy and cause discord. 'Tis nothing more than a shadow play of falsehoods."

"Yet shadows can only exist where there is light," Charlotte observed thoughtfully. "One must ask oneself why such stories find willing ears."

"An astute point, Miss Lucas," I conceded. "But let us not forget that the brightest of lights can cast the darkest of shadows."

"Are you implying that Mr. Wickham's grievances are

entirely without merit?" Elizabeth probed, a skeptical edge to her voice.

"Entirely," I affirmed, my intensity rising like a wave threatening to break. "His words are as insubstantial as mist, and I would stake my honor on proving the veracity of mine own character."

"Then perhaps, Mr. Darcy, you shall have to prepare yourself for such a defense, should the occasion arise," Elizabeth suggested, her lips curving into a smile that was neither mocking nor wholly serious.

"Perhaps," I echoed, allowing myself a small smile in return. "For now, I am grateful for the opportunity to present my case to such discerning individuals."

"Indeed, Mr. Darcy, we appreciate your candor," Charlotte said, just as she was beckoned by her mother from across the room. "If you will excuse me," she added with a polite dip of her head before departing.

"Miss Lucas is wise to heed her mother's call," I remarked, turning back to Elizabeth. "I would not wish to keep you from the company any longer than necessary."

"Your consideration is most appreciated, Mr. Darcy," Elizabeth said, her eyes lingering on mine for a moment longer than was customary. "And your defense, intriguing."

"Then perhaps we shall have the chance to continue this discussion at a later time," I suggested, feeling a glimmer of hope as the possibility of future discourse unfolded before me.

"Perhaps we shall," she agreed, the corners of her mouth lifting ever so slightly.

"Indeed, I—"

"Mr. Darcy! Lizzy!" The animated voice of Lydia Bennet pierced through our tête-à-tête like a misplaced note in a well-rehearsed sonata. Kitty trailed behind her, a wisp of a girl caught in the whirlwind of her sister's exuberance. Their sudden intrusion was like a cold dash of water upon the smoldering coals of our discourse.

"Lydia, Kitty," Elizabeth greeted them with a patient smile, though her eyes darted briefly to mine, echoing my silent plea for the resumption of our private conversation.

"Have you heard? There is to be dancing soon. You must promise us both a dance, Mr. Darcy!" Lydia declared, her curls bouncing with each word as she grasped my arm with the familiarity of a seasoned acquaintance.

"I– I would be most delighted," I responded with a measured politeness.

Lydia squealed with excitement and took hold of her elder sister's hands, tugging her toward the musicians. As the Bennet sisters were swept away by the renewed promise of merriment, I stood for a moment, watching Elizabeth merge back into the sea of guests.

With a sense of quiet optimism, I resolved to hold fast to that chance, nurturing the fragile hope that in time, Elizabeth might see beyond the rumors and Wickham's lies to recognize the man I truly was.

FIVE
elizabeth

AS I SAT QUIETLY in the corner of the drawing room at Lucas Lodge, I could not help but observe my dear sister Jane and Mr. Bingley sharing what appeared to be a most delightful exchange. The soft candlelight flickered across their faces, casting a warm radiance that seemed to enhance the growing connection between them. It was a scene of gentle mirth and unspoken attraction; subtle glances were exchanged, carrying with them the sweet promise of a budding romance.

Jane's gentle smile held a constancy, like the serene light of dawn, as she conversed with Mr. Bingley. It was impossible to miss the way his eyes lit up in her presence, reflecting a sentiment that needed no declaration. Their laughter mingled in the air – a duet of joy so harmonious it was as if their spirits had been acquainted long before this night.

"Miss Bennet," Mr. Bingley said to Jane, his voice brimming with an eagerness that betrayed his calm exterior, "I find myself entirely captivated by your thoughts on the beauties of Derbyshire. You paint such a vivid picture; I am almost convinced I can see the rolling hills and verdant valleys before me."

"And you, Mr. Bingley," Jane replied, the color rising ever so slightly in her cheeks, "have made the society of London sound so enchanting that I am tempted to brave the tumult of the city just to witness the spectacles you describe."

Their conversation flowed with ease, touching upon subjects from literature to landscapes, each remark from Jane met with an earnest nod or a spirited response from Mr. Bingley. There was a naturalness to their discourse that suggested a kinship of souls, and I found myself silently rejoicing in the genuine rapport blossoming before my eyes.

As the evening wore on, the pair seemed to exist in a world of their own making, surrounded by the hum of other guests yet isolated within their shared bubble of mutual interest. The compatibility between them was unmistakable, for they communicated not only with words but through a language of shared smiles and quiet understanding. And while the rest of us navigated the intricate dance of polite society, Jane and Mr. Bingley waltzed to a melody that only they seemed to hear.

In moments such as these, I could only hope that the fates would look kindly upon them both, guiding their affectionate friendship into something deeper, something lasting. For if ever two people deserved happiness, it was surely they.

The evening at Lucas Lodge continued with its usual blend of gaiety and whispered confidences, the latter often carrying more weight than the boisterous laughter that echoed through the opulent drawing rooms. In one obscure corner, where the candlelight did little to illuminate the gathered faces, Mrs. Bennet's voice carried a note of agitation barely veiled by her attempts at civility.

"Indeed, Mr. Bingley is as amiable as he is handsome," she remarked, her eyes darting towards the man in question, who was still deeply engaged in conversation with Jane. "Yet I cannot fathom his choice of acquaintance in that Mr. Darcy.

Such a notorious character, who seems determined to brood rather than partake in the celebration of life."

I observed Mr. Darcy from across the room, standing like a statue among merrymakers, his countenance solemn and his posture almost regal in its rigidity. The whispers about his wealth and status had done little to endear him to my mother, who saw only the shadow he cast upon Mr. Bingley's sunny disposition.

"Mama" I interjected softly, hoping to steer her away from outright criticism. "It is not our place to judge Mr. Darcy so harshly when we've hardly made his acquaintance. Perhaps his temperament is merely misunderstood."

Mrs. Bennet huffed, clearly unconvinced, but spared further comment as Mr. Collins approached, eager to offer another sycophantic remark about Lady Catherine de Bourgh's superior taste in dining chairs.

I took this opportunity to slip away, finding Jane momentarily unattended as Mr. Bingley had been called to confer with Sir William Lucas. Her eyes followed him as he walked away, the glow of affection unmistakable on her features.

"Jane," I began, leaning close to offer a semblance of privacy, "You seem quite taken with Mr. Bingley's company. Tell me, sister, does your heart flutter for him, or is it mere politeness that binds you to his side?"

A gentle blush crept up Jane's cheeks, a bloom so delicate and becoming that it could only be born of sincere emotion. "Lizzy," she replied with a hesitant smile, "I find Mr. Bingley to be most agreeable. His manners are so very pleasant, and he has been most attentive. But I must guard against being too forward in my sentiments."

"Dearest Jane," I said, warmth filling my voice, "Your cautious nature is both your strength and your shield. Yet do not let it blind you to the possibilities of happiness that dance before your eyes."

We shared a knowing glance, one that spoke volumes of the bond between sisters—a bond stronger than any words could convey. As we turned back to observe the room, I saw once more the tall figure of Mr. Darcy casting his gaze in our direction, his expression inscrutable. What thoughts lurked behind those watchful eyes, I could not discern, but they seemed, for an ephemeral moment, touched by a light I had not seen before.

* * *

THE MORNING SUN spilled across the breakfast table at Longbourn, casting a honeyed light on the assembled Bennet family. I watched as my mothers animated features alight with the fervor of fresh gossip, launched into a discours that had become all too familiar since our return from Lucas Lodge.

"Indeed," she exclaimed, her eyes wide and hands fluttering like sparrows in distress, "Lady Lucas was most explicit in her account of Mr. Darcy's disposition. It seems he has quite the reputation for haughtiness in society. Such arrogance! Can you imagine what influence he might exert on poor Mr. Bingley?"

"Ah," interjected my father, with his characteristic dryness, "And are these the same societies that find your nerves to be of the finest steel, my dear?" His keen eyes twinkled with suppressed mirth as he sipped his tea, entirely unperturbed by the discussion.

"Mr. Bennet!" Mama chided, though the effect was somewhat undermined by the flush of gratification at being the subject of conversation, even in such a teasing manner. "This is no laughing matter. We must consider Jane's prospects!"

I bit back a smile, knowing well the absurdity of the situation. The very man who could pose a threat to Jane's happiness was the same whose invitation to Pemberley lingered in my thoughts—a paradox not lost on me.

* * *

THE EVENING, as Jane and I readied ourselves for bed, the soft rustle of fabric and whisper of combs through hair provided a gentle backdrop to a more serious conversation.

"Jane," I began, hesitation coloring my tone, "do you recall our conversation on the rumors swirling about Mr. Darcy?"

She paused, the comb stilled in her hand, and met my gaze in the mirror. "Yes, Lizzy. I find them most troubling; surely Mr. Bingley would not hold such close company with a man undeserving of his friendship."

"True, but we cannot claim full knowledge of a man's character based merely on the company he keeps." I turned to face her, my concern reflected in her own clear, trusting eyes. "Mr. Darcy has invited me to visit Pemberley. I confess, I am eager to see it for myself—to perhaps understand the enigma that is Mr. Darcy."

"Visit Pemberley?" Jane's voice held a note of surprise, mingled with the quiet excitement that so rarely disturbed her placid nature. "But, Lizzy, would it be proper?"

"Accompanied by our aunt and uncle, propriety would be maintained," I assured her. "But, Jane, I would feel greater ease if you were to join us. Your presence would be both a comfort and a joy."

"Me?" Her countenance brightened with eagerness, before uncertainty once again dimmed her expression. "Oh, Lizzy, I wish to support you, yet I fear what impression it might give, should Mr. Bingley learn of it."

"Dear sister," I implored gently, reaching out to take her hand, "Mr. Bingley's regard for you is steadfast, I am certain.

And as for Mr. Darcy—well, we shall have to see what Pemberley reveals about the master of the house. Can I persuade you to accompany me?"

Jane stood silent for a moment, the tumult of her emotions playing softly upon her visage. At last, she squeezed my hand in assent. "For you, Lizzy, I will go. And perhaps," she added with a hopeful lilt, "we may discover a truth that will mute these disquieting whispers."

"Thank you," I said, relief flooding through me.

Together, we would face whatever mysteries awaited at Pemberley, armed with the courage that only sisters can bestow upon one another.

SIX
elizabeth

JANE and I admired the meticulously groomed gardens of Netherfield Park as I accompanied her to partake in tea with Mr. Bingley's sisters. My thoughts, however, were not on the pleasantries that awaited us but rather on the enigmatic Mr. Darcy and the unsettling tales told by Mr. Wickham. It was this curiosity, mingled with an indefinable sentiment, that propelled me towards Mr. Darcy when I espied him strolling along a shaded path lined with blooming roses.

"Mr. Darcy," I called out, affecting a casual air, though my heart quickened its pace at the prospect of our exchange.

"Miss Bennet," he replied, his countenance composed as he paused in his promenade. "To what do I owe the pleasure of your company?"

"I find myself desirous of conversation," I began, my voice steady despite the fluttering within. "Tell me, sir, what pursuits occupy your leisure?"

Darcy regarded me with a measured gaze before responding. "I am fond of reading and have an appreciation for the arts. And you, Miss Bennet?"

"Much the same," I said, allowing a touch of playfulness to

enter my tone. "Though I must confess to deriving particular enjoyment from exploring the many facets of human character."

"Indeed?" His eyebrow lifted in mild surprise. "A subject of great complexity."

"Most assuredly," I concurred, seizing the opportunity to delve deeper. "And one that often leads to profound reflection upon past actions, would you not agree?"

He hesitated momentarily, his expression unreadable. "Reflection is essential for any man who seeks to improve himself."

"Even if such reflections reveal decisions that might be construed as... questionable by others?" The words slipped from me, cloaked in innocence yet laced with implication.

Darcy's eyes met mine squarely, a flicker of vulnerability passing through them. "One cannot escape the scrutiny of society," he conceded. "Yet, it is often the case that the observer lacks full understanding of the circumstances that govern a man's actions."

"Perhaps then, enlightenment lies in discourse," I suggested, watching closely for his reaction.

"Perhaps," he allowed, and after a pause, he continued, "My responsibilities to family and estate are not light, Miss Bennet. To some, my choices may appear harsh, but they are made with the welfare of many in mind."

Listening to his words, I beheld the gravity with which he bore his burdens, and I could not but acknowledge the depth of consideration behind his demeanor. A man tasked with the care of an ancient name and the lives attached thereto surely faced trials beyond my ken.

"Family is indeed a sacred charge," I replied softly, sensing the sincerity in his voice.

"Indeed," he echoed, and in that moment of shared understanding, the rigid contours of his image seemed to soften.

As we returned to the main house, my mind churned with newfound insights into Mr. Darcy's character. The man I had deemed proud and unfeeling revealed a layer hitherto unseen, compelling me to question the veracity of my earlier judgments.

Upon our return to the parlor, I could not help but let my eyes follow Mr. Darcy as he navigated the small sea of guests with an air that spoke of both distinction and duty. His tall frame moved with a quiet grace that seemed at odds with the rigid set of his shoulders, a testament to the weight of his responsibilities.

"Lizzy," Jane whispered, drawing me out of my observations, "do you notice how kindly Mr. Darcy speaks to Miss Bingley, despite her constant provocations?"

"Indeed," I murmured, my gaze lingering on him as he offered a polite nod to Mrs. Hurst before turning his attention to a servant who had spilled a tray of cups. Rather than the expected chide, he afforded the young man a reassuring smile, instructing him gently on how best to avoid such accidents in future. It was a momentary glimpse into an aspect of his character that rumor had never touched upon, and it left me pondering.

The room was abuzz with idle chatter, but the care that radiated from his unexpected gestures sparked a curious warmth within me. Could it be that the man whom so many held in such high esteem was more than the sum of his reputed pride?

"Mr. Darcy is not at all what I expected," I admitted to Jane, my words laced with surprise.

"Nor I," she agreed with a soft sigh, her glance following mine.

As time drew on and our departure from Netherfield

approached, I found myself reluctant to leave without understanding the enigma that was Mr. Darcy. My previous convictions now seemed hasty, and I longed to unravel the layers of mystery surrounding him.

At length, we rose to take our leave, and I watched Mr. Darcy approach us with a countenance that bore signs of internal struggle. He appeared hesitant, his usual composure faltering slightly as he neared.

"Miss Bennet, might I have a word?" he asked, his voice low and somewhat unsteady.

"Of course, Mr. Darcy," I replied, excusing myself from Jane, who stepped aside with a knowing look.

"Miss Bennet," he began, "I must implore you to reconsider your opinion of George Wickham."

"Indeed, sir? And why might that be?"

The gentleman paused for just a moment, as though weighing his words carefully. "Mr. Wickham has deceived many with his charm," Mr. Darcy continued, his eyes searching mine for understanding. "His betrayal is not merely a personal affront but one that has caused great distress to my family."

"That is not what I have been told," I replied, but my tone was gentle and my curiosity was piqued. *Why would he decide to say such things?*

Mr. Darcy seemed taken aback by my words. "Of course, I do not know what I might say that might change your opinion, but I would urge you to take caution. Mr. Wickham is not what he seems—though he takes great pains to present himself to society in such a way as to make questioning his motives all the more difficult. He has always been this way."

I could not determine whether or not Mr. Darcy was being sincere. His tone was clipped and his stance was rigid, as though speaking to me about his former friend gave him great discomfort. My mind cast back to Mr. Wickham's affable ease and his comfort in speaking to me and my sisters–how different the two men were. But who could I trust in this instance?

"I see," I said. "Is there something else that you would wish to offer me as evidence against Mr. Wickham?"

Mr. Darcy took a breath and then shook his head. "I do not think so, Miss Bennet, it is not my place to speak of such things. I can only hope that in time, you will change your mind and see Wickham for the scoundrel I know him to be."

Without giving me a chance to speak, the gentleman bid me a good day and turned to walk away.

The sound of Mr. Darcy's retreating footsteps mingled with the rustling leaves, leaving a profound silence in their wake. I stood motionless, grappling with the jagged edges of my emotions. Could I have been deceived? Was it possible that the very man I had lauded for his easy manners and congeniality was capable of duplicity? *But what reason would Mr. Wickham have to lie?*

And by the same token, what reason would Mr. Darcy have to deceive me? But why, also would he seek to turn me against Mr. Wickham?

My fingers brushed lightly against the delicate fabric of my gown, tracing patterns as chaotic as the thoughts swirling within my mind.

"Lizzy?" Jane's gentle voice broke through my confusion.

"Mr. Darcy has... in all honesty, I do not know what he has done," I began, my voice barely above a whisper. "It seems that he wishes for me to reconsider my opinion of Mr. Wickham?."

Jane's brow creased with worry. "But what did he say?"

"Nothing at all," I replied. "And yet, so much at the same time– He said that there were things that I must know about Mr. Wickham, but that he was not the one to tell me of them– that it was not his place."

"Then who might we turn to?" Jane asked. "That is most confounding."

"Indeed, it is," I mused. "I can only hope that this mystery will unravel itself, but I do confess that I am most conflicted now in my opinion of both gentlemen. I find myself questioning much of what I thought I knew—about Mr. Darcy, about Mr. Wickham, even about myself."

As we made our way from the garden toward the carriage, the grandeur of Netherfield Park lay spread before us and my thoughts drifted back to Mr. Darcy, to the glimpses of kindness and consideration I had observed, so at odds with the aloof persona he presented to the world and, indeed, with the scandalous things that Mr. Wickham had told me about him. But what was I to do with such thoughts? And how could I bring order to this fresh chaos in my soul?

SEVEN
elizabeth

I WAS in the midst of a letter to my dear friend Charlotte when the maid brought in the post. My heart gave an involuntary leap as I recognized the seal and handwriting before breaking it open. The letter was from Mr. Darcy, and it renewed his invitation for Jane and I to visit Pemberley. For a moment, I felt an odd mixture of emotions—there was a flutter of excitement at the thought of seeing his fabled estate, but also a shadow of reluctance.

"Is it from Mr. Bingley?" Jane queried, noting, no doubt, the change in my countenance.

"From Mr. Darcy," I replied, feeling a curious tightness in my voice. "He has extended his invitation to Pemberley once more."

Her eyes widened with interest, yet I could not immediately share her enthusiasm. The specter of George Wickham's tales lingered in my mind, and I wondered if I was ready to step into the lion's den, so to speak.

"Will you go?" she asked softly, ever sensitive to the tumult that such a proposition might cause in my breast.

I hesitated, weighing the merits of curiosity against the

caution that propriety demanded. The contents of Mr. Darcy's letter seemed to anticipate my trepidation, as though he had divined my thoughts from afar.

"Mr. Darcy assures me he will not be present during our visit," I said, trying to mask the tumult within, "allowing us to view Pemberley without the... distraction of his company."

"Does that relieve your mind?" Jane pressed gently.

"Considerably," I admitted, and it was true. The assurance that I could roam the halls and gardens of Pemberley without fear of an unexpected encounter was a balm to my unsettled thoughts.

Yet even as I spoke, there was a part of me that chafed at the notion of being grateful for his absence. It was as though Mr. Darcy had laid down a gauntlet, challenging me to judge him anew, away from the whispers and prejudices that had colored our previous interactions.

"Then we should accept," Jane concluded with a smile, and I found myself nodding, almost against my will.

"Indeed, we shall." The words fell from my lips, sealing my fate.

What truly tipped the scales was not the grandeur of Pemberley or the prospect of a peaceful excursion with my sister, but rather the tantalizing possibility of uncovering the truth behind the enigma that was Mr. Darcy's past dealings with Mr. Wickham. Could the elegant rooms and verdant paths of Pemberley hold the key to understanding the man who had both insulted and intrigued me?

"Perhaps this visit shall shed some light on matters previously shrouded in mystery," I mused aloud.

"Whatever you seek, Lizzy, I hope you find it there," Jane said, her voice tinged with a warmth that bolstered my resolve.

With a newfound determination, I folded Mr. Darcy's letter and tucked it away. The die was cast, and I would venture forth to Pemberley, where either vindication or further vexation awaited. It was a peculiar sort of adventure, one that promised no dragons to slay nor treasures to unearth, yet it held the promise of something far more elusive—the chance to lay bare the truths of a man's character. And that, I decided, was a quest worth undertaking.

* * *

THE CARRIAGE ROLLED GENTLY along the graveled approach, and as the stately form of Pemberley came into view, I felt Jane's hand squeeze my own in shared wonder. The edifice before us was not simply a testament to affluence but rather a harmonious blend of man's creation with nature's grace. The stone façade rose majestically, its windows winking in the afternoon sun like a multitude of knowing eyes. The gardens unfolded around it, an embroidery of greenery stitched with vibrant blooms, while a placid lake mirrored the serene Derbyshire sky.

"Is it not everything you imagined, Lizzy?" asked Jane, her voice barely more than a whisper, as though she feared breaking the estate's enchantment.

"Indeed, it is more," I replied, allowing myself to be momentarily awed by the splendor that lay before us.

We descended from the carriage, our steps unhurried as we took in the vast expanse of the land that Mr. Darcy called home. My thoughts wandered to him—did this grandeur reflect the true disposition of its master? Or like the Greek statues adorning the gardens, did it mask a flawed humanity?

Upon entering the house, we were greeted by the housekeeper, Mrs. Reynolds, whose countenance bore such an expression of pride that it seemed an extension of the house itself.

"Mr. Darcy is absent, as per his letter," she confirmed, "but he entrusted me to extend every courtesy during your visit."

"Thank you, Mrs. Reynolds," said Jane, her gratitude genuine and warm as always.

As we were led through the halls, rich with paintings and the soft echo of our footfalls on marble, Mrs. Reynolds began to speak of Mr. Darcy with an affection that was palpable. Her anecdotes painted a picture of a man who, far from the aloof figure of society's balls and gatherings, showed great care for those who dwelled within his influence.

"Never have we known a kinder landlord, nor a gentleman of nobler character," she declared, and there was no mistaking the sincerity in her words.

"Indeed?" I found myself saying, my voice tinged with a curiosity I could not disguise. "It appears we had been previously misinformed about Mr. Darcy's disposition."

"Many judge Mr. Darcy too harshly at first," Mrs. Reynolds continued, "yet they know not his true nature. Why, only last winter, he provided new cottages for the tenants, refusing to let them suffer the cold. And he tends to the needs of all on the estate with a generosity seldom seen."

"Generosity and consideration seem to be the very essence of his character," Jane observed, a gentle reminder of her ever-present hopefulness in others.

I nodded, unable to refute the evidence of Mr. Darcy's virtues as presented by those who knew him best. As we walked through the halls of Pemberley, amid the echoes of past laughter and whispers of bygone secrets, I felt the rigid walls I had built around my opinion of Mr. Darcy begin to crumble. Could it be that I had been so swift to judge, to take offense where perhaps none was intended?

"Mrs. Reynolds, may I inquire about Mr. Wickham?" I

ventured cautiously, watching her face for any sign of discomfiture.

"Mr. Wickham?" she repeated, with a slight frown creasing her brow. "How do you know of him?"

"He has recently come to Meryton," I replied. "I know that he spent his youth here, and was a friend to Mr. Darcy–"

The housekeeper's expression hardened for just a moment. "Indeed, he was," Mrs. Reynolds said, "but his path led him away from this estate." A smile brightened her countenance once more. "Let us not sully this visit with talk of such unpleasantness."

"Of course," I acquiesced, though my mind was now awhirl with questions and doubts.

"Shall we continue our tour, Miss Bennet?" Mrs. Reynolds prompted, her smile inviting us further into the depths of Pemberley.

"By all means," I responded, stepping forward with a sense of anticipation.

Each room we entered, each tale of Mr. Darcy's quiet benevolence, added layers to my understanding of him. It was an intricate dance of perception and reality, and I found myself a willing participant, eager to learn the next step. As Pemberley revealed its secrets, so too did the enigmatic character of its master begin to unfold before me, challenging everything I thought I knew.

Jane and I strolled along the paths that wound through the gardens, our conversation light, yet thoughtful, as we reflected upon the revelations of the day. We had scarce rounded a bend adorned with blooms of vibrant peonies when the sound of carriage wheels crunching upon gravel reached our ears. Drawing near, we espied a carriage approaching, its elegant form befitting the grandeur of the estate.

"Surely," Jane murmured, "that must be Mr. Darcy's sister returning from Ramsgate."

"Indeed," I replied, my curiosity piqued. "I have long wished to make her acquaintance under circumstances less fraught with misunderstanding."

As the carriage drew to a halt before us, a young woman alighted, her petite frame moving with an unstudied grace that was at once endearing and imposing. It was none other than Georgiana Darcy herself, her expressive eyes—windows to a soul touched by innocence—scanning the surroundings before settling upon us. Her presence brought forth an air of youthful sophistication that seemed to harmonize with the tranquil beauty around us.

"Miss Bennet, Miss Jane," she greeted us, her voice a hushed melody, tinged with the hesitance of a fawn stepping into unknown terrain. She extended her gloved hand in a gesture both delicate and deliberate, like the unfolding of a blossom to the morning sun.

"Miss Darcy," Jane replied, taking her hand with warmth akin to a gentle embrace. "What pleasure it is to meet you at last."

"Indeed," I echoed, offering my own greeting. "Your home is quite remarkable."

"Thank you," she said, a blush coloring her cheeks as though praise were an unfamiliar companion. "I hope you will not think me too forward, but might I impose upon you both? You would honor me greatly by accepting an invitation to supper this evening."

"Miss Darcy, such an invitation could never be considered an imposition," I assured her, my heart softened by her genuine kindness. "We would be delighted to attend."

"Most delighted," Jane concurred, her serene countenance reflecting the sincerity of our acceptance.

"Then it is settled," Georgiana replied, her relief palpable as a summer breeze lifting the weight of apprehension. "I shall inform Mrs. Reynolds to expect us all at seven. There are so many things I wish to discuss with you both."

"Likewise," I affirmed, sensing beneath her timorous exterior a depth yet to be explored. "And perhaps, Miss Darcy, you might indulge us with a performance on the pianoforte?"

A shy smile flickered across her features, lighting up her visage like the subtle shine of twilight. "It would be my pleasure, Miss Bennet."

With a promise of the evening's engagement sealed between us, Georgiana excused herself to attend to her arrival matters, leaving Jane and I to continue our walk, our thoughts now occupied with the prospect of further communion with our hostess, and the unexpected blossoming of new friendship amidst the elegance of Pemberley.

EIGHT
elizabeth

WHEN WE RETURNED to Pemberly at the appointed time, the grandeur of Mr. Darcy's estate struck me afresh; its vastness and elegance seemed to dwarf our own modest home at Longbourn. Jane and I were ushered into the drawing-room where we were greeted once again by his sister, Miss Georgiana Darcy. She stood as a picture of youthful grace, her countenance marked by an endearing shyness that I could sense belied a warm heart.

"Miss Elizabeth, Miss Bennet," she said with a gentle voice that seemed to echo the harmonious melodies I had been told she so deftly played on the pianoforte. "So wonderful to see you both again, thank you for accepting my invitation this evening. My brother has written to me of you both. He holds you in high esteem." The hint of a blush stained her cheeks, and though her words were simple, their implication sent a flutter through my chest. What might Mr. Darcy have said of me?

"Indeed? Mr. Darcy honors us greatly with his good opinion," I replied, sharing a glance with Jane, whose smile was ever serene. Yet within, I could not still the tremor of curiosity as to the nature of his correspondence.

As we were led into the dining room, the candlelight lit the room with a gentle incandescence, illuminating the ornate furnishings, polished silver and the fine porcelain that graced the table. It was a setting befitting royalty, yet here we were but three, about to partake in a meal that promised culinary delights enough for a party twice our number.

"Mr. Darcy has always believed in the importance of dinner being a grand affair," Georgiana confided, her eyes gleaming with a mixture of pride and affection as she gestured towards the dishes before us. "He says it reflects not only on our family's standing but also on our regard for our guests."

"Your brother's hospitality is indeed most generous," Jane observed, as the first course—a delicate soup that carried the fragrance of fresh herbs—was placed before us.

"William... my brother, he cares deeply for Pemberley and all who reside within," Georgiana continued, her words flowing more freely as the evening wore on. "Even when he is away, he ensures that everything is just so."

"Such attentiveness speaks highly of his character," I noted, allowing myself a moment to admire the meticulous presentation of the roasted pheasant that followed, garnished with vibrant sprigs of rosemary.

"His letters are filled with inquiries about the household, and he never fails to remind me of the lessons he wishes me to practice," she added, her tone imbued with a reverence that spoke volumes of the bond between sibling and guardian.

"Your devotion to each other is truly commendable," I said.

Throughout the meal, an array of dishes danced upon our taste buds, each more exquisite than the last. Yet, despite the opulence, it was Georgiana's candid admiration for her brother that flavored the evening with a richness no dish could match.

"Georgiana," I ventured, as the savory sweetness of glazed carrots lingered upon my palate, "I am curious about your acquaintance with Mr. Wickham. He has been... a topic of many conversations in Meryton."

A shadow flickered across her face, like a cloud passing before the sun. Her countenance, which had been aglow with the warmth of familial pride, now appeared troubled.

"Mr. Wickham?" she echoed, her doe-like eyes widening ever so slightly. "How came you to know of him?"

Jane and I exchanged a glance, the understanding between us silent but profound. It was Jane who spoke first, her voice embodying the very essence of tranquility. "He resided in our neighborhood for some time and was well regarded by many. His manners have gained him the affection of Hertfordshire."

"Indeed," I added, folding my napkin upon my lap as I chose my words with care, much as one might select silverware from an array of polished cutlery. "However, it seems he has taken liberties with his account of events, particularly concerning his history with your family."

Georgiana's fingers trembled against the fine linen of her own napkin, her gaze dropping to her plate. "But what has he said?" she whispered, the softness of her voice belying the gravity of her inquiry.

"Amongst other things," I began, the weight of truth pressing upon my tongue, "he has imparted a most unfortunate tale of mistreatment at the hands of Mr. Darcy. He claims that he was denied a living promised to him and that he has suffered greatly as a consequence."

"Most grievous accusations indeed," Jane murmured, her blue eyes reflecting the candlelight and the sincerity within her heart.

The air seemed to grow heavy with silence, filled only by the gentle clink of silverware as Georgiana processed this unpleasant revelation.

Georgiana's countenance, once the picture of youthful

serenity, had clouded over with a storm of emotions. With a suddenness that startled both Jane and myself, she pushed back her chair, its legs scraping against the polished wood floor in a distressing cry.

"Please do excuse me," she uttered, her voice barely above a whisper, and with a swift turn of her skirts, she fled the room, leaving behind a palpable disquiet that hung in the air like the thick drapery adorning the grand windows.

"Georgiana!" I called out softly, yet she did not heed my plea. Without a further thought, I hastened from my seat, my heart pounding with a mix of trepidation and concern as I pursued Georgiana's retreating figure through the labyrinthine corridors of Pemberley.

"Miss Darcy," I implored as I finally came upon her slender form standing in the dimly lit hallway, her shoulders shaking with silent sobs. "I beg you, forgive my candor. It was never my intention to cause you such distress."

Georgiana turned to face me, her eyes brimming with unshed tears and a vulnerability that pierced my very soul. "Miss Bennet," she began, her voice quivering with an inner turmoil, "you are not to blame. It is I who should seek your forgiveness for the deception that has been so cunningly wrought by Mr. Wickham."

"Deception?" I echoed, my mind racing to comprehend the gravity of her words.

"Indeed," she replied, taking a deep breath as though steadying herself against the tide of confession. "Mr. Wickham... he sought to take advantage of my youthfulness, my naivety. He endeavored to persuade me to elope with him, spinning tales of love and adventure, all whilst his true aim was to claim my dowry."

The revelation struck me with the force of a winter gale, chilling me to the bone with its implications. Wickham, whom I had seen through a lens tinted by charm and conviviality, was but a shadow cast by the most nefarious of intentions.

"His words were honeyed, his manner so convincing," Georgiana continued, her hands clasped tightly together as if in prayer. "It was only by the grace of my brother's timely intervention that I was saved from a fate too dreadful to bear."

"Your brother?" I asked, my respect for Mr. Darcy augmenting with each passing second as I envisioned him the protector of his sister's honor.

"Mr. Darcy has always been my guardian, my champion against the cruelties of this world," she said, a note of fierce loyalty threading through her otherwise gentle tone. "He has borne much on my behalf, and for that, I am eternally grateful."

"Miss Darcy," I found myself uttering, moved by her plight and touched by her steadfast affection for her brother, "your trust in me with this information honors me more than words can express. I assure you, your confidence shall be met with the utmost discretion."

As we stood there in the dim corridor, a bond of shared secrets formed an invisible thread between us, I stepped forward and held Georgiana in a warm embrace as her tears flowed and her shoulders shook with light sobs. I knew that the truth of George Wickham must come to light. Yet, it must be done with care, for the sake of the hearts entwined in his web of deceit.

We stood together utterly motionless, my heart thundering against the confines of my chest as if to escape the tumultuous revelation. Mr. Wickham, a man whose charming countenance and smooth oratory I had once found so amiable, was in truth a scoundrel of the highest order.

"Elizabeth," she whispered as she stepped out of my embrace, "I—I cannot bear to think what others must believe of him."

"Nor I," I confessed, the words tumbling from my lips before I could marshal them. "To have been so deceived." My eyes, which had hitherto prided themselves upon their keen observation, now smarted with the sting of having been so thoroughly beguiled by falsehoods. The spark within them had dulled, replaced by a creeping frost of disillusionment.

"Forgive me," Georgiana said, her delicate features a tapestry of sorrow and apprehension. "I did not wish to cause you pain."

"Miss Darcy, it is I who should seek forgiveness," I replied earnestly, my resolve hardening amidst the newfound kinship blossoming between us. "Had I known the extent of Mr. Wickham's perfidy, I would have spared you the recounting of such distressing circumstances."

"Yet, knowing the truth allows for the possibility of healing," Georgiana suggested, a faint light igniting in her eyes—a shared understanding that acts as a salve to the wounds inflicted by duplicity.

"Indeed," I concurred, bolstered by her insight. Our fears and concerns regarding the unveiling of Mr. Wickham's deceit wove a thread of connection between us. It was a fragile bond, yet one fortified by mutual respect and the tacit agreement that honesty, no matter how painful its delivery, held power over deception.

"Elizabeth," Georgiana said, hesitantly reaching out a hand towards mine, "what are we to do?"

"Whatever is necessary to protect those we hold dear," I answered with quiet conviction, my fingers closing gently around hers. In this moment of solidarity, our spirits, though bruised, were united in purpose. We would face the repercussions of exposing Mr. Wickham's treachery together.

"Georgiana," I said quietly as we lingered outside the dining room door, "you must understand my apprehension. The consequences of laying bare Mr. Wickham's falsehoods could require your own presence, and seeing him again– There are those who would want evidence from your own lips."

Georgiana's eyes, large and luminous in the dim light of the corridor, met mine with an expression of profound concern. "I– I do not know if I could face him again."

"Indeed, it is a vexing predicament," I sighed, feeling the weight of the situation pressing upon me.

"Your wisdom in these matters far exceeds my own. I shall place my trust in whatever course you deem proper. My only wish is to see my brother's honor restored, though I shudder at the cost."

"Your faith in me shall not be misplaced," I assured her, touched by her confidence.

Together, we turned and reentered the dining room, where the soft glow of the candles danced upon the fine china and silverware, casting a warm ambiance over the still-laden table. Jane looked up from her seat, her countenance awash with sisterly concern.

"Forgive me for my abrupt departure," Georgiana said, reclaiming her chair with a composed air. "I found myself unwell, but Miss Elizabeth has been most kind in offering solace."

"Pray, do not distress yourself on our account," Jane replied with gentle sincerity, reaching across the table to bestow a reassuring touch upon Georgiana's hand. "We are, above all, friends here."

"Miss Bennet," Georgiana continued, her voice gaining strength, "it is with a heavy heart that I impart to you what I have shared with your sister concerning Mr. Wickham. It appears he is not the gentleman he has presented himself to be."

Jane listened with rapt attention as Georgiana recounted

the tale, her expression one of compassion mingled with dismay. When the telling was done, she nodded gravely. "Thank you for confiding in us. Rest assured, Elizabeth and I shall return to Hertfordshire equipped with the truth of your brother's character. His reputation shall be duly salvaged."

In that moment, the bond between us three ladies was like the finest silk—delicate yet unbreakable.

Though our conversation was renewed and the mood in the dining room lightened, I could not escape from the doubts and fears that clouded my mind. A confrontation with Mr. George Wickham lay ahead of us, and I could not determine how it would unfold, or what the repercussions of our actions would be...

NINE
elizabeth

WHEN JANE and I returned to our rooms at the Lambton Inn, the innkeeper's wife delivered into our hands a small package wrapped in brown paper.

Inside was a note from Georgiana detailing how she had discovered the papers in her father's study–papers and letters that she hoped would aid us in our confrontation with Mr. Wickham.

Jane and I looked through them breathlessly.

"Jane– I cannot believe it," I breathed.

"Notes about debts that were repaid," Jane said. "Small sums here and there, but here, Lizzy–a thousand pounds? So much?"

My lips pressed into a thin line as I looked over the faded ink. Mr. Wickham's trail of deceit, every vice he had attributed to his former friend, all laid bare for us to see.

"Here lies not merely ink and paper, but the means to unmask Wickham's duplicity," I declared.

"Indeed, Lizzy," she responded, her voice the gentlest whisper, "it does seem so, but will it be enough?"

"We cannot allow his falsehoods to go unchecked, especially now that they threaten the happiness of those dearest to us. If Mr. Wickham was, indeed, up to no good here in Lambton, we should be able to find someone who can attest to it."

"In the morning we shall seek it out," Jane said. "I am certain that Mrs. Long will be able to assist us."

"Indeed, I do hope so," I said. "My mind is greatly troubled, and I cannot see a way forward—"

"Take heart, Lizzy," Jane said with a smile. "I believe we shall find what we are looking for."

* * *

AS THE MORNING dawned bright and cheery, I found that I had to force myself to match its brightness. The weight of everything we had learned was heavy upon my shoulders and the trouble that awaited us when we returned to Hertfordshire was something I very much wished that I could avoid.

But I could not. This injustice had to be met head on.

As we stepped outside in search of Mrs. Long, the freshness of the day lifted my spirits somewhat. The streets of Lambton were abuzz with the daily toils of its inhabitants. Shopkeepers heralded their wares with gusto, while children darted between stalls like sparrows in flight. We navigated this tapestry of life with a singular focus: to seek out those who might unveil the true character of George Wickham.

Our path led us to the back garden of the inn, where Mrs. Long, the innkeeper's wife, was hanging out the washing to dry in the morning sun.

Her acquaintance with local affairs was as well known as the reputation of her establishment. She greeted us with a warm smile, yet I could detect a hint of reservation behind her hospitable facade.

Her eyes, sharp and discerning, flickered with a curiosity

that spoke volumes. "Miss Elizabeth, Miss Jane, what brings you to my garden this fine day?"

"Mrs. Long," I began, adopting a tone of earnest inquiry, "we find ourselves in need of your unique insights. You are, without doubt, a fount of knowledge concerning the comings and goings in Lambton."

"Mr. George Wickham," continued Jane, her melodious voice lending gravity to the name. "We are given to understand that he was once familiar with Pemberley and its environs. Any recollection you might share would be of great service."

Mrs. Long regarded us for a moment, the gears of remembrance turning within her mind. "Mr. Wickham, you say? A charming gentleman, though I dare say not without his...peculiarities."

Her circumspection was palpable, yet I sensed that beneath her reticence lay a wellspring of information that could prove invaluable. It was a matter of coaxing it forth with the subtlety and grace that the situation demanded.

"Any peculiarities in particular that come to mind?" I pressed gently, allowing my own curiosity to imbue my words with a touch of intrigue. "Even the most trifling detail may cast light upon the truth we seek."

Mrs. Long's expression softened, and it seemed as though the floodgates of her memory had been opened. With a glance exchanged between Jane and myself, I knew that we stood on the cusp of revelations that would shape the course of our endeavor. And so, armed with fortitude and the support of sisterly affection, we listened intently, poised to discern the threads of veracity amidst the tangled weave of Wickham's past.

With a warm smile from Jane and an attentive nod from myself, Mrs. Long appeared to find solace in our company.

"Mr. Wickham did have his way with words," she began,

her voice tinged with a reserved disapproval that suited her station as innkeeper's wife. "But there were whispers, you know—whispers that his charm was oft employed to less than honorable ends." She glanced about as if the very walls might betray her confidence. "During his time at Pemberley, it was said he borrowed more than just books from the library."

"Indeed?" I probed, tilting my head in an unspoken gesture of encouragement. "And these borrowings... they were not solely of the literary kind, I presume?"

"Far from it, Miss Bennet," Mrs. Long replied with a sigh. "There were matters of money involved. Debts left unpaid, promises broken. A gentleman in deeds but not, perhaps, in actions."

Jane and I exchanged a look of understanding. The pieces of the puzzle concerning Mr. Wickham's character—or lack thereof—were fitting together with alarming clarity.

"Your candor is most appreciated, Mrs. Long," Jane said softly. "We are indebted to your willingness to share such insights."

"Think nothing of it, Miss Bennet," Mrs. Long replied, though I detected a trace of relief in her voice as we took our leave.

Our next course led us to the office of Mr. Phillips, whose reputation for thoroughness in legal matters was well known in the village. Upon our entrance, Mr. Phillips looked up from a stack of papers, his countenance all business.

"Miss Elizabeth, Miss Jane," he greeted us, setting aside his work with a practiced efficiency. "To what do I owe this unexpected pleasure?"

"Good day, Mr. Phillips," I returned with a respectful incline of my head. "We seek enlightenment on a certain matter involving one Mr. George Wickham."

"Ah," he responded, his brow knitting ever so slightly. "A name that has crossed my desk one time too many."

"Indeed?" I asked, my curiosity piqued by his foreboding tone.

"Mr. Darcy, of Pemberley, found it necessary to settle a rather unsavory account on Mr. Wickham's behalf," Mr. Phillips divulged, his words precise and void of any embellishment. "It was a matter of some delicacy, for the sum was not insignificant, and the creditor quite impatient."

"Mr. Darcy paid Wickham's debts?" Jane echoed in surprise.

"Quite so," Mr. Phillips confirmed. "Though it is not my place to conjecture upon the motivations of gentlemen, one might surmise it was done to preserve the dignity of Pemberley—and possibly to prevent further disgrace upon Mr. Wickham."

"Your insights are most valuable, sir," I said, my mind already turning over the implications of this revelation. "I thank you for your forthrightness."

"Think nothing of it, Miss Elizabeth," Mr. Phillips replied with a nod. "It is always a service to ensure the truth is known."

As Jane and I stepped out into the cobblestone street, the gravity of our findings weighed heavily upon us. Yet, within that weight lay the power to mend the fabric of reputations torn asunder by deceit. The day's inquiries had yielded a basket brimming with unsavory truths about Mr. Wickham, truths that now clamored for exposure.With resolve fortifying our spirits, we turned homeward, determined to weave truth back into the tapestry of our lives.

"Jane," I began, my tone tinged with the weight of our predicament, "we possess the means to unveil Wickham for the scoundrel he is, yet we must tread lightly. Our every step affects not only our family but the felicity of your future with Mr. Bingley."

Jane's countenance, ever serene, now mirrored the concern

that furrowed her brow. "Lizzy, I am well aware that our dear mother's disdain for Mr. Darcy has become entwined with her opinion of Mr. Bingley. She sees them as one and the same since that dreadful affair with the rumors." Her voice, though soft, carried the unmistakable note of distress.

"Indeed," I replied, my mind racing with strategies to untangle this intricate web without harming Jane's prospects. "We must confront Mr. Wickham directly, armed with what we have learned. Yet such a confrontation could further embroil Mr. Bingley if not handled with the utmost care."

"Would that we could rely on the good sense of everyone involved," Jane sighed. "But Mama's feelings are not easily swayed by fortune when her principles, however misguided, are roused."

"Which is why," I said, coming to an abrupt halt beside a hedgerow abloom with roses, "we ought to seek counsel from Papa. His judgment will be crucial in determining how best to proceed."

Jane nodded, a grateful smile playing upon her lips. "Yes, let us return to Longbourn and lay before him our discoveries. Papa's insights will no doubt shed light upon this thorny path."

* * *

THE EVENING SHADOWS stretched across the verdant lawn of Longbourn as we made our approach, the house standing as a testament to the many confidences it had kept within its walls. Upon entering the drawing-room, where my father was ensconced behind his newspaper, the familiar scent of leather and ink greeted us like an old friend.

"Ah, Lizzy, Jane," said Papa, lowering his paper with a practiced ease that revealed nothing of his thoughts. "I trust your foray into Lambton has been productive?"

"Indeed, Papa," I began, sharing a glance with Jane, whose quiet resolve bolstered my own. "We bring news concerning Mr. Wickham that is of considerable import and we are in need of your guidance."

As I laid out the evidence, piece by measured piece, upon the mahogany desk, my father's sharp eyes flickered with interest. "Commendable work," he mused, steepling his fingers. "Yet I urge you to tread carefully. Your mother's censure of Mr. Bingley and Mr. Darcy is loud enough to wake the dead. It would not do to throw Jane's prospects into disarray."

"Nor would we wish it," Jane interjected, her calm voice a soothing balm. "But surely the truth must be brought to light lest others fall prey to Mr. Wickham's deceit."

Mr. Bennet sighed, the corners of his mouth twitching in a reluctant smile. "Wickham has been calling here, paying marked attentions to Lydia and Kitty—with your mother's enthusiastic blessing, no less. One shudders to think what mischief they might entertain under such encouragement."

A chill ran through me at the thought of our youngest sisters embroiled in Wickham's schemes. Jane's hand found mine, a silent vow passing between us.

"Then we must act with both resolve and discretion," I declared, feeling the weight of the path ahead. "For the sake of all whom we hold dear."

"Indeed," Mr. Bennet acknowledged. "And quickly so. The web of lies is already spun—and who knows how soon it may entangle us all."

"Thank you, Papa," Jane said, her gaze steady and unwavering. "Your counsel is, as ever, invaluable."

"Go, then," he replied with a nod.

We withdrew from the drawing-room, the door closing softly behind us. As we traversed the dimly lit corridor, the portraits of our ancestors watched in silent judgment, their eyes seeming to follow us as we passed.

"Jane," I whispered, my voice barely audible above the soft creaking of the floorboards, "we have but one course now—to confront Mr. Wickham before he does further harm."

"I am with you, Lizzy," Jane affirmed, her hand gripping mine with a strength that belied her gentle appearance. "Together we shall face this tempest. And should the seas prove rough, we shall weather them as we always have—side by side."

Our resolve set, we ascended the staircase to devise our strategy. The task ahead loomed daunting, yet there was a certain thrill in the knowledge that the power to mend or mar lay within our grasp. Together, with truth as our ally, we would bring to light the shadows that threatened to stain the honor of our family.

TEN

darcy

I HAD TRAVERSED the length of Netherfield's drawing room so often that the very pattern of the carpet seemed indelibly etched upon my mind. Each step was a measured tempo in the symphony of my unrest, and with every turn, I felt the sharp sting of society's invisible whip upon my back.

"Confound it all," I muttered under my breath, halting to gaze out of the window. The verdant landscape of Hertfordshire offered no solace to the tumult that raged within me. A squirrel darted up the trunk of an ancient oak, blissfully ignorant of the complexities of human affection or the rigid structures imposed by noble birth.

My thoughts, invariably drawn towards Elizabeth Bennet, were both torment and delight. In her presence, I found a vivacity that quickened my pulse, a wit that challenged my own, and eyes that seemed to see through the façade I presented to the world. She was sunlight piercing through the overcast sky of my existence, and yet, the very brightness of her being cast the shadows of doubt deeper into my soul.

"Elizabeth," I whispered, allowing myself the luxury of speaking her name aloud. It rolled off my tongue like a sacred incantation, imbued with the power to unsettle my most guarded emotions. My fingers absently brushed through my hair, as turbulent as my thoughts.

How could I reconcile the fervor of my love with the impropriety of expressing it? How could I, Fitzwilliam Darcy, scion of an esteemed lineage, dare to indulge in the fantasy of uniting my life with a woman whose connections, though respectable, would be deemed insufficient by my peers?

Yet, to be near her was to feel alive in a manner I had never known, and to be apart from her was akin to exile from the very essence of life itself. What cruel trick of fate it was to find one's heart ensnared by one so likely to refuse it!

The societal expectations that had been my constant companions since birth now appeared as insurmountable walls, casting long shadows over the path to happiness. Yet the strength of my affection for Elizabeth made even the prospect of scaling such barriers seem a worthy endeavor.

Can reason be folly when the heart leads one to uncharted territories? I pondered, the weight of my station momentarily lifted by the effervescent notion of pursuing what many would deem impossible.

In this moment of solitude, with naught but my restless thoughts for company, I vowed to confront the morrow armed with nothing less than my sincerest intentions.

The warmth of the hearth did little to soothe the cold tendrils of apprehension that wound themselves around my heart. As I stood before the expanse of the drawing room window at Netherfield Park, my gaze fixed upon the rolling expanse of the estate beyond, a heavy sigh escaped me. The scandal concerning Wickham was akin to a tempest on the horizon, threatening to upend all that I held dear.

Surely, I thought, *the taint of such an association would not merely cast a shadow upon my own reputation but sully the very name of Bennet.*

The mere notion of Elizabeth entangled in this unsavory narrative caused a tightness in my chest. To imagine her countenance, marked by distress at the prospect of society's censure, was unbearable.

Would she suffer the indignity alongside me? Or would the fear of ostracization from her kin and our peers compel her to retreat? For it was known all too well how unforgiving society could be towards those who dared step outside the bounds of propriety. And Wickham, with his nefarious charm, had woven a web that could ensnare us both in disgrace.

"Mr. Darcy, a letter for you, sir," the butler's voice interrupted my thoughts and offered a brief reprieve. Taking the envelope, I recognized the elegant script at once—Georgiana. A flutter of hope stirred within me as I broke the seal.

"Dearest Brother," it began, and with each line, my spirits lifted. Georgiana detailed the events of Elizabeth and Jane Bennet's visit to Pemberley with such clarity and warmth that it was as if I had been amidst their company. Her kind words painted a portrait of Elizabeth that was all admiration and affection—a testament to her character that I knew only too well.

"Charles," I called out, eager to share the fortuitous news with my friend who was equally embroiled in matters of the heart with Miss Jane Bennet. Bingley entered the room, his countenance brightening immediately upon seeing the letter in my hand.

"From Georgiana?" he inquired, leaning forward with palpable interest.

"Indeed it is," I said. "As I had hoped, my dear sister Jane."

"Happy news, indeed," Charles said with a smile. "If your

sister holds them in such high regard, surely the rest of our acquaintance will follow suit."

"Perhaps," I conceded, allowing myself a cautious smile.

"If she has spoken to Georgiana, then surely she will know the truth about Wickham—"

"I hope that to be true," I replied.

"Will you visit her? To know her mind?"

"I believe I must," I said. I could not wait for Elizabeth to come to Netherfield Park, but though I did not wish to press the issue—I needed to know what her feelings might be, and if her mind had been changed by Georgiana's gentleness and the truth of what had happened to her.

* * *

THE CHILL of the early morning air bit at my cheeks as I mounted my steed—a noble chestnut with a gait as smooth as glass. The fog lay thick upon the meadows, the rising sun but a muted glow behind the veil of mist. We set off at a brisk canter, the rhythmic pounding of hooves against the damp earth resonating like a drumbeat heralding the gravity of my intentions.

As we rode, the world awakened around us. The dew-laden grass shimmered with the touch of dawn's tentative light, and the fragrance of damp earth mingled with the sweet scent of blossoming hawthorns. A lark took flight from the hedgerow, its song piercing the hush of morning—a melody of freedom and anticipation.

By the time Longbourn came into view, my heart had taken up the cadence of the ride—fast and unyielding. I dismounted with a flourish, handing the reins to a stable boy who appeared, bleary-eyed and tousled from sleep. My attire bore the marks of haste and travel, but there was no time for vanity. As I approached the house, I noted the windows aglow with the soft light of candles, casting a welcoming warmth against the stone façade.

"Mr. Darcy," greeted the maid who answered my knock, surprise etched upon her features.

"I apologize for the early hour but is Miss Elizabeth available? I must speak to her with haste." I asked.

"Yes, sir, if you will follow me to the drawing room."

The chamber was familiar, yet I felt like an interloper, the weight of my impending confession turning the very walls into silent judges. I had barely begun to pace when Miss Elizabeth entered the room—the woman who occupied my every thought. Elizabeth Bennet stood before me, her countenance composed, yet her eyes betrayed a guarded curiosity.

"Mr. Darcy," she said, inclining her head slightly. "To what do I owe the honor of this early morning visit?"

"Miss Bennet," I began, finding my voice amidst the torrent of my emotions. "I have come to inquire... Have you uncovered the truth of Mr. Wickham's character?"

Her gaze did not waver. "I have, indeed, and it is most grievously different from what I was led to believe."

"Then, I must speak plainly," I continued, stepping closer. "My affection for you has defeated all judgment. The heart is not so easily directed; it will not be governed by propriety or society's dictates. In defiance of every obstacle, my admiration and love for you has only increased." My words were a fervent whisper, a truth laid bare. "Elizabeth, would you do me the great honor of consenting to be my wife?"

In the silence that followed, every heartbeat was a thunderous echo in my ears, the fate of my future happiness hanging precariously in the balance.

Elizabeth's eyes, wide with a blend of astonishment and incredulity, searched mine for sincerity—their usual spark of vivacity momentarily dimmed by the gravity of my entreaty. Her lips parted as if to speak, yet no words found passage. The very air around us seemed to hold its breath, awaiting her response.

"Mr. Darcy," she at last whispered, her voice scarcely carrying above the soft rustle of leaves outside the parlor window, "this is...most unexpected."

The muscles in her slender throat moved visibly as she swallowed, betraying the rapid pulse I could see fluttering at the base of her neck. With a hand that trembled ever so slightly, she reached out to the back of the nearest chair, not to take a seat but to steady herself against the swell of emotions I had unleashed.

"Your proposal is of such a nature," Elizabeth continued, her gaze now dropping to where her fingers gripped the chair's carved wooden frame, "that it requires a great deal of consideration." She lifted her eyes once more to meet mine, searching, probing for an anchor in the storm I had stirred.

"Indeed, sir, the challenges we are likely to endure should not be taken lightly. There is the matter of my family's inferior connections and the scandal surrounding Mr. Wickham," she said, her voice gaining strength even as it wavered with vulnerability. "I must consider what acceptance might entail, not only for myself but for you as well."

The weight of her scrutiny was as a crucible testing the mettle of my resolve. Yet, within the crucible's fire lay also the promise of a future I yearned for—one that would defy convention and withstand the winds of adversity.

"Miss Bennet," I implored, stepping nearer though careful not to encroach upon the delicate space between us, "I am acutely aware of the obstacles before us. But I assure you, my intentions are guided by neither whim nor fleeting fancy. My regard for you is steadfast. If you would consent to be my wife, together we shall rise above the whispers of society and forge a path defined by our mutual respect and affection."

Her countenance, a canvas of internal debate, softened at the edges as the corners of her mouth dared a hesitant smile—a dawning awareness of the sincerity that fueled my plea. And yet, the furrow of her brow spoke of the struggle within: the balance between caution and desire, pragmatism and passion.

"Mr. Darcy," Elizabeth said, her voice steadier now but tinged with the weight of consequence, "you ask me to contemplate a decision that could alter the course of our lives irrevocably."

"Indeed, I do," I replied, my own heart thrumming with the intensity of the moment. "For I believe that life—shared with you—would be a far richer journey than any other."

We stood thus, locked in a tableau of anticipation, the world beyond the paneled walls of the parlor fading into insignificance. Time itself seemed to hang in the balance, each tick of the mantel clock a drumbeat in the symphony of our intertwined fates.

ELEVEN
elizabeth

MY HEART WAS A TUMULTUOUS SEA, each wave crashing against the resolute shore of my reason. Mr. Darcy's eyes bore into mine, an expectant silence enveloping us both.

"Miss Bennet," he began, his voice as steady, "if you find it in your heart to grant me the honor of calling you my wife, know that every day henceforth would be devoted to your happiness."

My breath hitched, and I felt the world narrow to the space between us. All my previous misgivings seemed to evaporate.

"Mr. Darcy," I finally spoke, my voice barely above a whisper, betraying the storm of emotions within, "I have been blind to the true depth of your character, swayed by shadows and misconceptions. But now, seeing you, truly seeing you, I am convinced of the nobility of your soul. Yes, I will accept your hand. It is with a heart full and unequivocally open that I consent to be your wife."

A surge of elation transformed his austere features, and the corners of his eyes crinkled in a rare display of unguarded joy.

He stepped closer, the distance between us diminishing until I could feel the warmth radiating from him.

"Elizabeth," he said, his use of my given name a caress more intimate than any touch, "your acceptance bestows upon me the greatest joy. I vow to cherish you, to stand steadfastly by your side regardless of what adversities we may encounter. Together, there is no storm we cannot weather, no obstacle insurmountable."

"Your words, Mr. Darcy, fill me with great joy," I replied, allowing myself to indulge in the comfort of his nearness. "And I, too, shall stand by you with equal resolve and sincerity."

The air around us seemed to shimmer with the unsaid and the yet-to-be. We were two souls, once at odds, now converging on a path woven by threads of respect, understanding, and burgeoning love. Each glance, each word exchanged, fortified the bond that tethered us.

* * *

I CARRIED the secret of my engagement to Mr. Darcy like a precious treasure held close to my heart. I wished to tell everyone of what had happened, but until Mr. Wickham had been thwarted, I could do nothing and tell no one, and for the moment I had sworn Darcy to secrecy until such time that he could be vindicated.

The assembly I had been dreading, now loomed ahead of us as an opportunity to reveal Wickham's crimes to all those who had been taken in by his lies.

As Jane and I prepared for the festivities, we discussed how our plan would unfold–but it was impossible to know what might occur, or how Mr. Wickham would react to our discoveries...

The assembly room of Meryton, resplendent with the glow

of wax candles and the harmonies of a string quartet, bore witness to the gaiety of its occupants. A kaleidoscope of silk and satin gowns swirled in time to the music, punctuated by the precise steps of their partners. Yet amidst this tableau of merriment, my heart wrestled with a disquiet that lay heavily upon it.

Jane and I found Wickham engaged in idle conversation near the refreshment table, his countenance the very image of untroubled ease. At our approach, a flicker of trepidation crossed his visage, quickly masked by a practiced smile. I wondered if he had heard of our visit to Pemberley from one of my sisters, but I could not be certain.

"Mr. Wickham," I said , "we have come to confront you on a matter of honor and integrity."

"Miss Bennet! Miss Elizabeth!" he exclaimed, feigning surprise. "To what do I owe this unexpected pleasure?"

"Your charade ends tonight, sir," I said sharply and loudly for all to hear. Nearby conversation stilled and the musicians abruptly stopped playing their instruments. "We are in possession of evidence that will expose your falsehoods and restore Mr. Darcy's reputation."

Wickham's eyes darted about, seeking an avenue of escape or perhaps an ally, but none would meet his gaze. "Evidence?" he echoed, his composure faltering as beads of perspiration dotted his brow.

"Indeed," I affirmed. "You have woven a tapestry of deceit, ensnaring those I hold dear. Your actions have threatened the wellbeing of my sisters, and for that, you shall be held to account."

"Let us not make a spectacle," Wickham implored, his voice lowering to a whisper of desperation. "Surely we can discuss this in private?"

"Your duplicitous words have been whispered in too many

willing ears," Jane retorted. She drew forth a small selection of letters we had discovered in Lambton from her reticule and presented it to Wickham, who recoiled as if the very ink bore an accusatory glare. "These letters, penned by your own hand, reveal your true intentions and the depth of your malice. Your debts. Your lies. And your attempt to ruin Mr. Darcy's only sister for financial gain!"

A collective murmur arose among the gathering crowd, their attention now fixed upon the unfolding drama. Wickham, cornered by the incontrovertible proof of his transgressions, stood bereft of the charm that had once been his shield and sword.

"Miss Jane, Miss Elizabeth," he attempted, his voice tinged with a hint of his former confidence, now rapidly eroding. "Surely we can come to an understanding?"

"An understanding was beyond your reach the moment you chose deception over decency," I countered, my gaze locked with his. "Your falsehoods are laid bare for all to see."

As the evidence mounted and the assembly beheld the unraveling of George Wickham, it became clear that the esteem he had so cunningly cultivated was now forfeit. With each accusation substantiated, his fate was sealed, and the ballroom, once a stage for his deceptions, had become the court of his reckoning.

"Is there not a single soul who will stand by me?" Wickham's voice, once the melody of every salon and parlor, was now but a discordant note hanging in the perfumed air of the ballroom. His imploring gaze swept over the assembly, searching for an ally amidst the sea of stern faces.

"Stand by you?" Mama cried, whose previous admiration for Wickham had been as fulsome as it was misplaced, echoed with scorn. "One might as well stand on the edge of a crumbling cliff and hope not to be cast into the sea."

"Mr. Wickham," Lady Lucas chimed in, her tone laced with disappointment, "we welcomed you into our homes, our hearts... and this is how you repay our generosity? With lies and machinations?"

The murmurs amongst the crowd grew louder, a chorus of disillusionment that filled the grand ballroom where once music and laughter had reigned. Even as Wickham attempted to weave his explanations, each word seemed to tighten the noose of evidence around his neck.

"Please!" he implored, an edge of desperation cutting through his usual smoothness. "Consider the possibility of a misunderstanding—"

"Mr. Wickham," Colonel Forster interrupted, his military bearing giving weight to his words, "the evidence is most compelling. Your 'misunderstandings' stretch far beyond the limits of credulity."

"Indeed," added Sir William Lucas with an authoritative nod. "A gentleman would own up to his mistakes, not persist in falsehoods!"

The very air in the room felt charged with the electricity of revelation, as if the gilded mirrors and flickering candles bore witness to Wickham's fall from grace. The once-charming officer stood isolated, the cold shoulder of society turned firmly in his direction.

"Miss Bennet," Lady Lucas whispered, her voice barely reaching my ears above the din of collective shock, "to think we were all taken in by such a man! And poor Mr. Darcy—to think that we all believed the worst of him!"

"Indeed," I said. "He has borne Mr. Wickham's grievances with admirable restraint."

As the assembly absorbed the finality of Wickham's disgrace, the whispers transformed into a resounding call for justice. No longer able to hold their tongues, the people of

Meryton vocalized their censure, casting Wickham out from their midst like flotsam from a tempest-tossed ship.

"Leave Meryton, sir," bellowed one of the officers, his voice carrying the weight of the community's verdict. "We will not harbor a deceiver amongst us."

"You will admit your wrongdoings," I cried. "Confess—Confess that all of the lies you have told about Mr. Darcy have been your own misdeeds!"

I–" Mr. Wickham's face, one I had once found handsome, paled with fear. But instead of a confession, the letters Jane had given him fell from his hand and dropped to the floor.

Wickham, bereft of allies and sanctuary, had no recourse but to retreat. With a final glance that bore the vestiges of his shattered charm, he turned on his heel and made for the exit, his departure from the ball—and Meryton—a sullen capitulation to his fate.

At a sharp command from the Colonel, two officers, formerly Wickham's close companions, gave chase, intent on bringing him back to the garrison for punishment.

With Wickham's retreat, a hush descended upon the ballroom, a collective breath held and then released in a sigh of communal relief.

"It seems that we owe Mr. Darcy a long overdue apology," Sir WIlliam said with a harrumph. "Is he here tonight?"

It was then that Mr. Bingley and Mr. Darcy entered the assembly rooms, and I wondered if they had seen Wickham as he dashed for the exit.

A smile broke over my face as I turned to Mr. Darcy, my heart buoyant with the victory that had been so dearly won.

"Mr. Darcy," I began. "You have come at just the right time–We have prevailed in the most extraordinary manner."

"Indeed, Miss Bennet," he replied, his eyes meeting mine with an intensity that spoke of the tumultuous journey we had weathered. "Elizabeth," he corrected himself, his use of my name sending a shiver of intimacy through the space between us. "I cannot put into words my gratitude–."

"Yet, I must confess," I continued, the joy of our success overshadowed by a burgeoning sense of contrition, "I have wronged you greatly—even beyond the grievances laid at Wickham's door. I judged you harshly, and allowed his falsehoods to cloud my perception, and for that, I am truly sorry."

"Your apology, while appreciated, is unnecessary. Our understanding of one another was marred by misconception on both sides. Let us look not to the missteps of the past, but forward to the path we now tread together."

The music from the orchestra began once again, filling the room with a melody that seemed to celebrate the turning of the tides. In that moment, amidst the grandeur of the ballroom, we stood as two souls aligned, our hearts brimming with hope for what was yet to come.

Laughter, warm and genuine, rippled through the crowd, their eyes softening as they beheld Mr. Darcy's uncharacteristic display of humility. The vestiges of prejudice, once so deeply entrenched in the minds of Meryton's citizens, seemed to dissolve under the weight of truth and sincerity.

"Elizabeth," he said, the use of my given name sending a shiver of delight through the room, "our journey henceforth will be one charted by honesty and affection. I vow to stand beside you, not only as your partner but as your most ardent advocate."

"Your promise is reciprocated in full, Fitzwilliam," I declared, the syllables of his name tasting of promise and anticipation on my tongue. Our hands met, clasped in a union that spoke volumes more than any grandiose gesture could convey.

As the musicians struck up a lively tune, our loved ones gathered around us, their expressions painted with relief and jubilation. With each note played, the shadows of our past grievances receded further into memory, giving way to the vibrant hues of hope and love.

"Mrs. Bennet," Mr. Darcy addressed my mother with a respectful nod, "might I have the honor of claiming the first dance with your daughter? For it seems only fitting that we celebrate our mutual felicity with the merriment such news deserves."

"Mr. Darcy!" she exclaimed, her voice rising above the music, "You have ever been the most attentive of gentlemen! Pray, lead my Lizzy out, and let the joyfulness of your hearts be reflected in the elegance of your steps!"

And so, under the watchful eyes of a community whose sentiments had transformed from suspicion to celebration, Mr. Darcy and I commenced a dance that was more than mere formality—it was the manifestation of two souls reconciled, a declaration of a future envisioned together. Our movements were graceful, yet charged with an energy that bespoke the depth of our connection, our shared laughter a melody harmonizing perfectly with the orchestra's tune.

Meryton, once a place of turmoil and conjecture, now bore witness to the dawning of our happiness—a happiness built on the cornerstones of love, forgiveness, and the unwavering conviction that, united, we would forge a path brimming with contentment and light.

THE END

more from blue flowers press

A Turn of Fate

The Brighton Affair

Darcy's Duty

A Change in the Wind

A Storm Over Pemberley

Saving Georgiana

A Race to Love

A Certain Unhappiness

A Daring Heart

A Gentleman's Folly (Duet)

A Suitable Arrangement

The Tenacious Miss Bennet

Elizabeth's Misplaced Memories

A Lady's Price

Elizabeth, Enchanted

Mistakenly, Darcy

A Ruined Woman

Rescuing Pemberley

Elizabeth, Adrift

The Daring Miss Bennet (Duet)

Milton Keynes UK
Ingram Content Group UK Ltd.
UKHW050159250624
444652UK00014B/558